Sports Illustrated KIDS

GOODNIGHT SOCCER

BY **MICHAEL DAHL** ILLUSTRATED BY **CHRISTINA FORSHAY**

PICTURE WINDOW BOOKS
A CAPSTONE IMPRINT

Beneath the pink clouds and a sunset of gold . . .

The stadium's packed. Every seat has been sold.

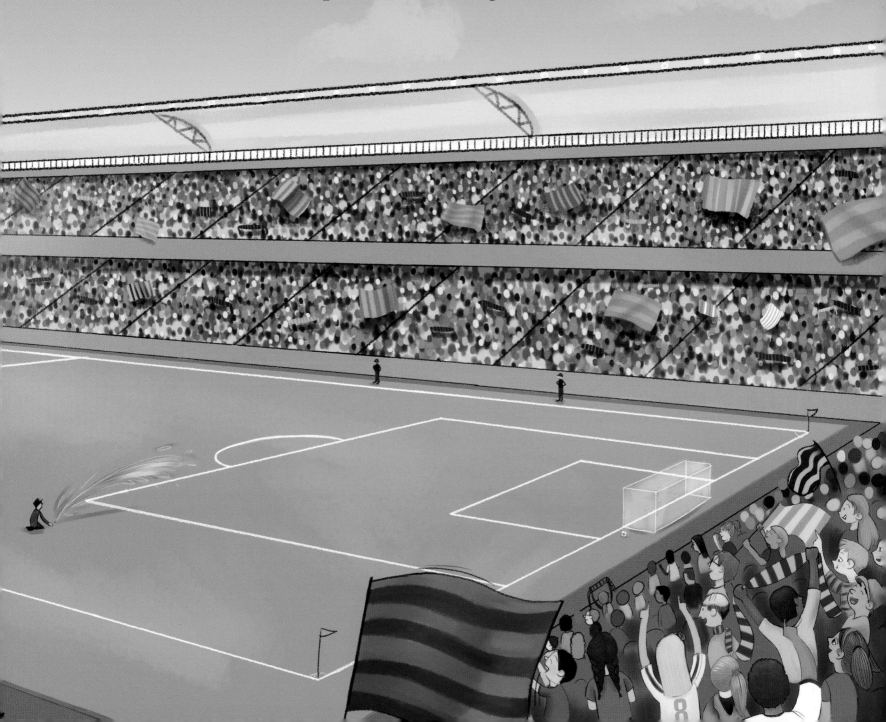

The crowd is excited.
We're all chanting and singing.

We wave our bright scarves, and the stadium's ringing.

Our team wins the toss. Here's the kick from our foes.

The ball leaves the circle —
now watch where it goes!

Dribbling
and passing,
our forwards
move fast.

Then our
strikers zoom in
when the defense
is passed.

Soon, a kick! And a goal!
We jump, and we roar!

But the other team rushes
and captures a score.

Through the game, the ball flies.
Watch it bounce! Watch it bend!

The clock keeps on ticking . . . Oh, how will it end?

Then a penalty kick
somehow slips through a hole.

Hits the back of the net!
It's a last-second . . .

Now over the scoreboard, we see stars in the sky.

Too soon, the game's over. Too soon for goodbyes.

THANK YOU, FANS!

2-1

Goodnight, captains. Your teams are the best!

Goodnight to you,
coaches.
Now your players
can rest.

Goodnight, infielders. Goodnight, strikers and backs.

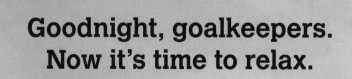

Goodnight, goalkeepers.
Now it's time to relax.

Goodnight, net.
Goodnight, ball.

To the fans in their jerseys,
goodnight to you all.

Goodnight, field where our team was the winner.

Goodnight, bright lights,
getting smaller, growing dimmer.

Goodnight to my heroes. My champion team.

Goodnight, soccer.
Hello, dreams.

TO **BARB,**
REMEMBERING ALL THE FUN AND SOCCER GAMES

Published by

PICTURE WINDOW BOOKS
a Capstone imprint
1710 Roe Crest Drive, North Mankato, Minnesota 56003
www.mycapstone.com

Cataloging-in-Publication data is available on the Library of Congress website.

ISBN: 978-1-62370-833-7 (hardcover) • ISBN: 978-1-5158-0870-1 (library binding)
ISBN: 978-1-5158-2559-3 (eBook PDF)

Designer: Bob Lentz

Printed and bound in the United States of America.
010824S18